HOT WHEELS™

Volcano Blast!

By Ace Landers
Illustrated by Dave White

SCHOLASTIC INC.

New York   Toronto   London   Auckland
Sydney   Mexico City   New Delhi   Hong Kong

ISBN 978-0-545-20870-3

12 11 10 9 8 7   10 11 12 13 14 15/0

Printed in the U.S.A.   40
First printing, February 2010

Welcome to Volcano Island.

The cars will race inside the volcano!

The finish line is at the top!

The ground begins to shake.

The race begins!

The cars drive at full speed.

The race is tight!

The cars hit the ramp
and launch into the air.

Some cars do not make it
into the cave.

Watch out for the pool of lava!

The lava is rising.

The racecourse is steep.
Rocks fall on the road!

The yellow car gets hit.

The lava leaps into the air!
It can destroy the cars.

The racecars are burning rubber!

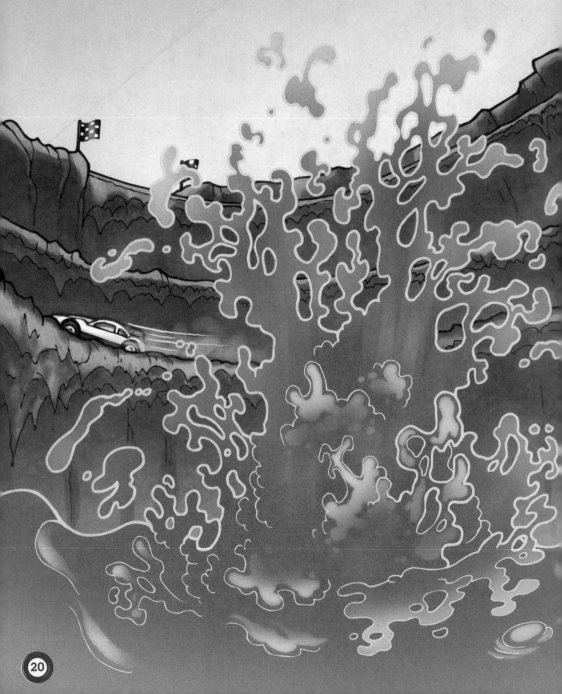

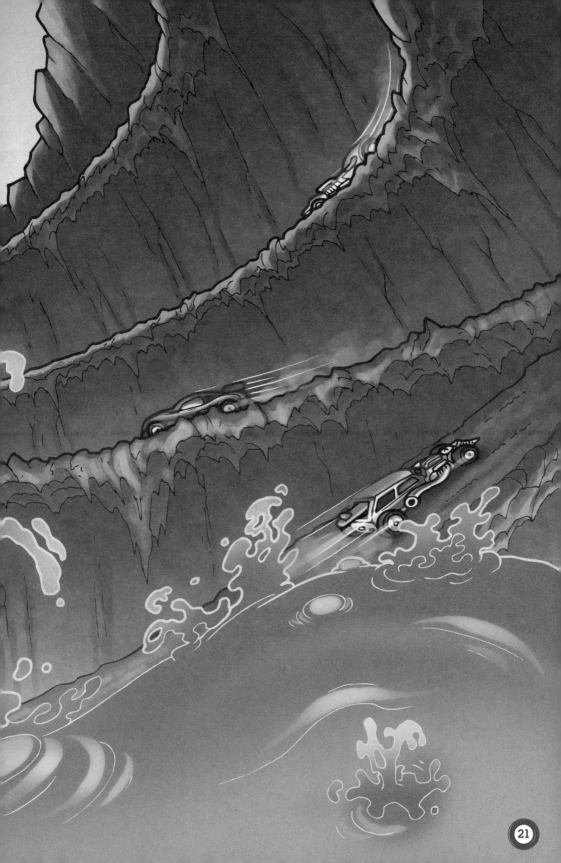

The lava is getting close.

The blue dune buggy is trapped!
It is out of the race.

Other cars are gaining
on the green car.

The red car hits the green car.

The red car breaks free.

It is hard to see the finish line.
There is too much smoke.

The volcano erupts.
The cars fly into the air!

Who will win?

The green car wins!

What a blast!